T0209238

Keri Funk

WESTBOW
PRESS®
A DIVISION OF THOMAS NELSON
& ZONDERVAN

WestBow Press books may be ordered through booksellers or by contacting:

WestBow Press
A Division of Thomas Nelson & Zondervan
1663 Liberty Drive
Bloomington, IN 47403
www.westbowpress.com
1 (866) 928-1240

ISBN: 978-1-5127-9167-9 (sc)
ISBN: 978-1-5127-9166-2 (e)

Library of Congress Control Number: 2017909771

Print information available on the last page.

WestBow Press rev. date: 6/26/2017

I want to dedicate this book to my husband who pushed me to get it done, editing it for me, and to publish it. I want to thank my mom, grandmother, and mother in-law for reading parts of it and giving me feed back. Also for my best friend Mal for reading parts of my book and all the girls from bible study for begin supportive. Thanks to all.

Contents

Chapter 1
This is Rebecca

Once there was a little girl named Rebecca. Rebecca didn't have a mom or a dad, so she lived in a house with other kids that didn't have moms or dads. Miss Kathy toke care of all the children. Rebecca loved Miss Kathy, but she longed for a mommy and daddy of her own. Every night Miss Kathy told them that one day they would have a family to call their own. Every night Rebecca dreamed of getting her own mommy and daddy, but since she was thirteen, she didn't think it was possible. When Rebecca felt alone and sad, she loved to read books about faraway lands where kings and queens lived. She also loved to read about a land where animals talked just like people. But her favorite books were love stories, where two people fell in love and got married. Since Rebecca was at the age where most kids don't get adopted, she couldn't wait to find a nice boy to marry one day. Together, they would create the family she never had but always wanted.

Rebecca's Dream

One night Rebecca had a dream unlike any of the ones she had before. That dream changed her life forever. Three nights ago, before she went to bed, she wrote a letter. The letter was for a couple who was looking for a child to adopt. Miss Kathy told the children to write a letter about themselves to the couple, who would read the letters. They would pick a few children to come see and then pick one to adopt. Even though Rebecca believed she wouldn't be the one chosen, she wrote a letter anyway and, this is what it said,

> Dear Mommy and Daddy,
>
> My name is Rebecca Keller, and I am thirteen years old. My birthday is June 10th. I have long, light-brown, hair and hazel eyes. Depending on what I wear my eyes change color. When I wear white or periwinkle, my eyes even turn purple. I love animals. My favorites are cats, dogs, horses, and bunnies. I love to read, write, ride my bike, shop, color, and take care of and play with animals. My favorite colors are purple, pink, light blue, and yellow. My favorite places to go are the mall, and the beach. My favorite foods are pizza, mac and cheese, cheese cake with cherry

topping, and sherbet. I don't like pickles, tomatoes, hot dogs, and chili. I like to collect rocks and seashells. My favorite holidays are Christmas and Halloween; I love dressing up in a costume every year. I love to watch World of Wonder movies. Well, I believe that is everything about me.

Sincerely,
Rebecca Keller

The next day the couple came to pick up the letter. And early the next morning, they made their decision of three kids they wanted to see and spend time with. To her surprise, Rebecca was one of them. But even though she was chosen, Rebecca still figured they wouldn't choose to adopt her.

When the couple came to pick up Rebecca they asked her to pick where she would like to go. "I would like to go to the mall," said Rebecca.

At the mall, they bought Rebecca a brand-new outfit for the summer. She chose a bright pink shirt with flowers on it and bright pink shorts.

"I can't remember the last time I had a new outfit," exclaimed Rebecca. "Miss Kathy always gave us donations or hand-me -downs from older kids in the house."

"Well I'm glad that we could give you something new and nice for the summer," said Joy, the mother in the couple as she hugged Rebecca.

Over the next two days, Joy and her husband, Wayne,took the other two kids out to spend time with them. Even though Joy and Wayne had been very nice to her and bought her a nice outfit, they bought the other two kids something too, so she figured she wouldn't get picked again. Sadden, Rebecca went to sleep not knowing she would wake up a different girl.

Chapter 2
Naranet

Rebecca suddenly woke up in a strange land. As she started to walk around, she saw strange animals and strange people. Some of these she remembered from a movie she once saw, but others she had no clue what they were.

She went over to an elf and asked, "Excuse me sir, but where am I?""You are in Naranet little one," he replied.

"Sir, please don't call me little, I am thirteen," said Rebecca, not wanting to be rude.

"Oh I'm sorry young girl. You looked smaller than that age," apologized the elf.

"That's ok. I've often have been told I look younger than I am," said "Sir, I don't know where to go. I'm not from here."

"Well, young lady, first you need to know where you want to go," said the elf.

"I don't know where I should go."

"Then come with me. We can go to the market. Then you can meet my friend Downer."

"I'm guessing Downer is an elf like you."

"Yes he is an elf. But he sees the negative in everything, which is why we named him Downer," explained the kind elf.

"Oh, I used to be like that when I was younger. You see, I'm an orphan. I don't have a mom or a dad."

"Oh, I'm sorry to hear that. Now instead of calling me 'sir,' you can use my name which is Hepter." said the elf. "Then instead of calling me young lady you can call me Rebecca." Said Rebecca.

On the way to the market, Rebecca couldn't believe how different this place was from her own world. The trees talked, danced, and sang. The animals talked and walked just like people.

"This place is very different from home," said Rebecca as they walked to the market.

"What do you call where you come from?" asked Hepter.

"I call it home for now, since I don't have a family. I live with a woman named Miss Kathy. She is nice."

"What I meant is what is the name of the city or village," said Hepter as he sat down on a rock to rest.

"The name of the city is Decksville."

"That is an interesting name for a village," said Hepter as he stood up. "We should keep going to the market."

Finally, after about two hours of walking they make it to the market.

"This is nothing like I thought it would be. It's so small. It's like the farmer's market back home," exclaimed Rebecca when she saw the market.

"So I guess your markets are bigger back home-- except for these things you call farmer's markets," replied Hepter.

"Well, yeah a lot bigger. Like four times this big. The farmer's markets are as big as this one. They sell fruits and vegetables," explained Rebecca as she took in the sights of this small market.

Then all of a sudden Hepter yelled, "There is Downer. Come on Rebecca!" Hepter grabbed Rebecca's arm as he ran over to Downer. "Downer, my dear friend, how are you this fine day?" Hepter asked.

"Fine day? What is so fine about it?" Downer sounded very grumpy. "I see what you mean about him being negative about everything," said Rebecca with a little giggle.

"Yes, Downer just can't seem to find a silver lining in anything. Now that I think about it, he wasn't always like that."

"Are you telling me there was a time when Downer wasn't a downer?" .

"Yes Rebecca, he used to be a wonderful man and friend," Hepter answered. "Would you like to hear the tale of what happened?"

"I would love to," answered Rebecca.

"Well, like I said, Downer was a wonderful man. The nicest elf you would ever want to meet. He had a very pretty wife and two beautiful children, a boy and a girl. His wife and children were everything to him, then the accident happened."

"What kind of accident?" asked Rebecca.

"It happened about ten years ago," Hepter started. "That day started out just like any other day with a trip to the market. We saw each other at the market and then the unthinkable happened. It isn't there anymore, but there used to be a huge pond about a mile from here. The two kids wanted to go swimming, so they sneaked away to go swimming. When we noticed the kids weren't with his wife, her name was Vernet, we started to look for them. When we found them swimming in the pond we were relieved that we found them and that they were okay. Then all of a sudden, Downer's daughter started to scream; her name was Cassnet. She was screaming 'cause her brother, his name was Downet, had gone under. Cassnet was younger and wasn't strong enough to pull her brother from the water to save him, but she stayed in the water, not wanting to leave her brother's side. When Vernet found us at the pond, even though she couldn't swim, she jumped in, trying to save her son. Then, after his wife jumped in, his daughter loss her footing, slipped, and went under. Downer and I couldn't swim. All we could do was stand there and watch his wife and children drown."

"I don't really know what to say. I never knew anybody who lost their wife and kids all in one day," said Rebecca with tears in her eyes. "You see I never knew my parents. My mom gave me up for adoption right after I was born, and no one has ever wanted me."

"I'm sorry Rebecca, if I had ever married and was younger I would adopt you, but I never found the right elf to marry and now I'm an old elf," explained Hepter, "I will say that you are very beautiful. It is hard to see why you never found a family."

"I guess I was never good enough for anyone to love me."

As Rebecca huddled down to cry, Naranet and Hepter faded into the background. When Rebecca looked up she was back in her bed at Miss Kathy's house, then she fell back to sleep and soon was in a beautiful new world.

Chapter 3
World of Wonder

This new world was a place Rebecca loved very much. She saw characters from her favorite movies. The first person to talk to her was her favorite character Sapphire.

"Why hello there young girl, what is your name?" asked Sapphire.

"Hi, my name is Rebecca Keller," replied Rebecca.

"Well Rebecca, welcome to the World of Wonder, where all the characters from all the Wonder movies live," said Sapphire.

"I love Wonder movies. I have seen almost all of them," said Rebecca.

"Well then, I guess you know who I am?" asked Sapphire.

"Of course, you are Sapphire, my favorite Wonder princess," exclaimed Rebecca.

"Well thank you, Rebecca, I am flattered," said Sapphire as she shook Rebecca's hand.

"Sapphire, I know we just met but may I please have a hug?" asked Rebecca, trying to be a polite.

"You seem like a very nice girl, and you are very pretty so yes," said Sapphire as she hugged Rebecca.

That hug was one Rebecca would remember for the rest of her life and it made her feel great.

"Would you like to meet some more characters from Wonder movies?" asked Sapphire.

"Would I? Yes! Of course I would!" exclaimed Rebecca, just about ready to jump out of her skin.

Next, Sapphire took Rebecca to see someone who also from the same movie as Sapphire was.

"Rebecca, this is Aaron, from all three of the movies that him and I are in," said Sapphire as Aaron shook Rebecca's hand.

"It is an honor to meet you, Aaron I loved all three of your movies," said Rebecca, star struck.

"Trust me, Miss Rebecca, the pleasure is all mine. It is always a pleasure to meet a fan," said Aaron.

"Come on Rebecca, there are more people I want you to meet," said Sapphire as she took Rebecca by the hand.

"Now right over there, in that little house, is where the seven elves live, but they aren't home at the moment," explained Sapphire.

"Even though the elves aren't home, is Red Rose home?" asked Rebecca, as she listened to see if she could hear Red Rose singing.

"No Rebecca, she lives in a castle with the prince she fell in love with," said Sapphire.

"Oh that's right, now I remember," exclaimed Rebecca.

"Listen," whispered Sapphire "I hear the elves coming home."

"I would love to meet them. Can we?" asked Rebecca, almost giddy with excitement.

"Of course we can. Lets go," said Sapphire, as they walked towards the elves' cottage.

As the elves walked toward their cottage Sapphire called out to them.

"Elves, come meet a visitor to our land. Rebecca this is-"

"No need, I know who they are," said Rebecca as she interrupted Sapphire.

"This is Shy, Surgeon, Silly, Cheerful, Drowsy, Allergy, and Angry," exclaimed Rebecca, very excited to meet the elves.

After she talked with the elves for a bit she and Sapphire walked on. After about two miles they came upon a castle that Rebecca recognized, it was the castle or Keri and David.

"Sapphire, I know this place. I saw it in my favorite movie" exclaimed Rebecca.

"Good, then you know who lives here," stated Sapphire as they walked into the rose garden. "They spend a lot of time in the rose garden, Keri loves roses," explained Sapphire.

"I like roses too," stated Rebecca as they walked pass a rose bush.

"Now I wonder where Keri and David are?" Sapphire asked out loud. "Keri! David!" cried Rebecca when she saw them come around the corner.

"Keri and David, this is Rebecca, she is visiting our world, and is a big fan of your movie," explained Sapphire.

"Well that is wonderful, we always love to meet our fans," said Keri as she stuck out her hand to shake Rebecca's.

"It is so wonderful to meet you. I have watched your movie sixty times," said Rebecca, shaking from excitement.

"Well, I must say you are what we would call a super fan," said David.

"May I pick a rose to take with me?" asked Rebecca in a timid voice.

"Why of course you can, pick any one you like," David and Keri said at the same time.

Once Rebecca picked a rose, she and Sapphire walked on to another castle, one Rebecca didn't recognize.

"Sapphire, I don't recognize this castle. Who lives here?" asked Rebecca as she gazed up at the castle.

"This is Tara's castle," answered Sapphire.

"That was my favorite movie when I was very little, because the rest of the World of Wonder movies scared me," confessed Rebecca.

"Look over there, Tara is looking over the garden," said Sapphire as she led Rebecca over.

"I always wondered if she really kept mice for pets?" asked Rebecca.

"Well no, they made that up for the movie," said Tara, who had heard Rebecca talking.

"I hate mice. They are gross, but I loved the song we had them do."

"Is Prince Tyler here too?" asked Rebecca.

"Yes, he is inside if you would like to meet him? I can take you in," answered Tara.

"Sapphire, do I have time to meet him?" Rebecca asked.

"Sure, I will come in too," replied Sapphire.

"Honey, we have company," Tara called as they entered the castle's main room.

"Well hello Sapphire. Who is your friend here?" asked Prince Tyler.

"Honey, this is Rebecca. She loved our movie as a little girl," Tara answered.

"All the other World of Wonder movies' villains scared me," said Rebecca in a shy voice.

"Tara, Prince Tyler, we have had a wonderful time, but Rebecca and I need to get going. We have two more people for her to meet," explained Sapphire.

As Rebecca and Sapphire left the castle Rebecca started to wonder who she was going to meet next. As they walked up to the next castle Rebecca recognized it right away.

"Sapphire, this is where Prince Jason and Alice live," exclaimed Rebecca.

"Yes it is, and our last stop on your tour for World of Wonder," stated Sapphire.

As they walked toward the castle, Rebecca was excited to meet Alice and Prince Jason. Once in the court yard Sapphire called out for Alice.

"We are over here Sapphire," answered a voice that Rebecca knew very well.

"Alice!" yelled Rebecca as she ran in the direction of the voice.

When she saw Alice and Prince Jason she stopped short, because she remembered they didn't know her even though she had known them her whole life.

"Alice, Prince Jason, this is Rebecca. She is a fan of World of Wonder movies," said Sapphire as she introduced Rebecca.

After an hour of talking to Alice and Prince Jason, Sapphire and Rebecca had afternoon tea with them. After tea, Sapphire suggested they head back to her palace.

Once they got back to Sapphire's palace she said, "Well I'm going now, but you will be fine."

"Where are you going?" asked Rebecca, afraid of being left alone.

"Aaron and I are going for a ride on our flying dragon," said Sapphire.

Less than five seconds later, Sapphire climbed on a flying dragon. While Rebecca waved goodbye to Aaron and Sapphire, World of Wonder faded and Rebecca was back in her bed at Miss Kathy's.

Chapter 4
World of Colors

When Rebecca awoke again she was in a world unlike anything she had ever encountered before. A world where the colors were so vibrant. The flowers, sunsets, the siding on the houses, and the cars were all her favorite colors. Even her clothes had changed and were her favorite colors. Everywhere she looked she saw something else that was one of her favorite colors. The sunset was every shade of purple, pink, yellow and light blue Rebecca could imagine. All the flowers were all shades of her favorite colors. She just couldn't believe this world was real. Every house had siding, and each one was a shade of one of her favorite colors. This world also had the most beautiful rainbows Rebecca had ever seen. She was so busy looking at everything that she nearly knocked down a small girl.

"Hi, my name is Chloe," said the little girl.

"Hello, my name is Rebecca. Sorry for almost knocking you down," apologized Rebecca.

"It is fine, you seemed interested with everything," said Chloe, not understanding why Rebecca was so interested with everything.

"Well, everything here is amazing. Everything is one of my favorite colors. Also, I'm just a visitor here," explained Rebecca.

"Well then, first of all welcome to World of Color. Let me explain why everything here is one of your favorite colors. No matter where anyone looks, here they see one of their favorite colors. That is why everything here is one of your favorite colors," explained Chloe.

"Wow! This world is really magical!" exclaimed Rebecca.

"Would you like me to show you around?" asked Chloe.

"I would love that." answered Rebecca.

As they walked through the town, Rebecca still couldn't believe that she saw the colors purple, pink, light blue, and yellow everywhere.

"So Chloe, what colors do you see when you look around?" Rebecca asked.

"Well, I see red, white, and blue," replied Chloe.

"Wow! I just can't believe that I only see my favorite colors," said Rebecca looking at everything. "This is like my dream world."

"I'm glad you like it here. I always wanted a sister," said Chloe.

"Chloe, I'm not staying here. At some point I will need to go back to where I come from," explained Rebecca.

As Chloe started to cry, Rebecca realized that everything except the people's faces were her favorite colors even Chloe's tears were light blue.

"Chloe, I'm sorry but I don't belong here. I must go home," said Rebecca as she tried to hug Chloe.

"I hate you. I want you to leave now!" shouted Chloe as she pushed Rebecca away.

"I don't know how to get home. When I was in the other worlds I didn't get to chose when I left, it just happened," explained Rebecca.

Then she told Chloe about the other worlds she had been too.

"So I'm stuck with you for a while?" asked Chloe.

"Yes, I will be here for a while, and I don't know when I will be leaving. It will just happen," answered Rebecca.

"I guess while you're here we can have fun," said Chloe.

"Ok, do you have a beach or a mall we could go to?" asked Rebecca.

"We have the red, white, and blue beach. At least that is what I call it since I see everything in red, white, and blue," explained Chloe.

"I would love to see this beach. The beach is my favorite place back home," explained Rebecca as they started off to the beach.

"This is the best beach in the World of Colors. I go here almost every day," said Chloe as they neared the shore line.

"Don't you go to school?" Rebecca asked her.

"My parents thought it best to home school me because of my heart murmur. In case something would happen, and homeschooling meant I didn't have to do gym." explained Chloe.

"So your parents just let you come here by yourself?" asked Rebecca. "Sort of, our house is right over there. My mom can see me from the kitchen window. She is the teacher and a stay at home mom. My dad owns his own company, but he can't do his CEO job from home so he goes to an office everyday of the week except Saturday and Sunday," explained Chloe.

"So I guess you don't get to see your dad much?" asked Rebecca.

"He comes home every day at five-thirty, so he is home for supper every night," explained Chloe.

"That must be nice for you and your family to have him home every night," said Rebecca as she looked out to the ocean.

"Rebecca, do you have any brothers or sisters?" Chloe asked as she walked towards Rebecca.

"I don't remember if I do or not. I was very young

when I was taken from my mother," said Rebecca as she continued to look at the ocean.

"All I have is a baby brother, he is only four months old, and he is a pain. He cries almost all the time. I always wished I would get a sister, but mom and dad said they aren't going to have any more kids," Chloe stated.

"The other kids I live with at Miss Kathy's house, they have become kind of like my brothers and sisters. We are like one big family. Sure, sometimes we fight and get upset with each other, but at the end of the day we love each other," Rebecca explained to Chloe.

"Do you ever think about looking up your real mom and asking if you have any real brothers and sisters?" Chloe asked.

"Maybe, I mean I have thought about it. I would also want to know why she gave me up, but I think I want to wait to find her until I'm older. I'm only thirteen," said Rebecca as she looked out to the ocean again.

"Rebecca, what color do you see when you look at the night sky?" Chloe asked as she looked up to her new friend.

"I see a dark, rich purple streaked with medium, light blue," said Rebecca.

"I wish I knew what that looked like," Chloe sighed.

"Chloe, you get to see your whole world in the

colors you love so what is wrong?" asked Rebecca putting her arm around Chloe.

"It gets boring seeing the same three colors day after day. I mean, in your world you see every color there is. I only see three colors. It gets boring. I wish I could see all the colors of the world," cried Chloe as she sank to her knees on the beach.

Rebecca helped Chloe up and then they walked to Chloe's house. As they were walking towards the house Chloe's mother ran towards them.

"Is she ok? What happened?"asked her mother in a panic.

"Mom, I'm fine. I just got upset for a minute. I'm fine. I want you to meet my new friend, Rebecca, can she join us for supper?" Chloe asked.

"Sure honey, now you and Rebecca go in and wash up for supper," said Chloe's mother as they went into the house.

"I wonder what we are having for supper," said Rebecca and she and Chloe washed their hands.

"Most likely something very healthy. Mom makes me eat healthy because of my heart," explained Chloe.

"So she makes everyone eat healthy just because you have a heart murmur?" Rebecca asked Chloe.

"She says that if I eat healthy my heart will stay healthy longer," said Chloe as they walked to the kitchen. "So mom what is for supper?"

"Well, your father and I figured we can have

something unhealthy every once in a while, so we got pizza for supper," said Chloe's mom.

"I like pizza. Does it at least have meat on it this time?" asked Chloe.

"Yes, it is not veggie pizza like we had for your birthday," explained her mother, "Rebecca, do you like pizza?"

"I love pizza!" exclaimed Rebecca as they sat down to eat.

After Chloe's dad said grace, they passed the pizza around and started to eat.

After Chloe finished her pizza she asked, "Mom, what are we having for dessert?"

"Your favorite, dirt pudding with gummy worms," said her mom as she went to get the pudding.

After supper was over, Chloe asked her mom if Rebecca could spend the night.

Her mom said, "It is fine with us as long as her parents don't mind."

"She doesn't have parents and she is a visitor here," explained Chloe.

"Ok, then she can stay overnight we will blow up the air mattress for her to sleep in your room," said her mom as she went to ask Chloe's dad to blow up the mattress.

After her shower, Chloe and Rebecca said their prayers and right before she went to sleep Chloe said, "I hope you are not gone in the morning."

"Just know I had the best time with you, but I also hope I get to stay longer too," said Rebecca then they both fell asleep.

In the morning Chloe woke Rebecca up just as the sun started to rise. The sky was just beautiful, with light blue, streaked with pinks, light purple, and yellows. Before Rebecca could climb out of bed, the World of Color started to fade

"Chloe, I'm leaving, you are fading!" exclaimed Rebecca.

Right before everything left, Chloe hugged her and Rebecca closed her eyes. When she opened them again the World of Colors, and Chloe, were gone and she was at Miss Kathy's.

Chapter 5
Island of Animals

When Rebecca woke, she was laying on a beach with the ocean just a few feet away. She knew right away that it was not the same beach she had just left since it wasn't purple, pink, or light blue.

As Rebecca got up and looked around to try to figure out where she was, she saw animals everywhere. There were a couple weird things about the animals she noticed when she saw them. First off, she noticed that they were wearing clothes just like people did, and second the animals talked just like people do."

*What is going on here?"*Rebecca thought as she walked passed all the animals.

Rebecca decided to walk back to the beach since she loves beaches. It was a beautiful day. The sun was shining, blue sky, warm, and little breeze blowing. The water was moving with the breeze, and the sand looked like it shimmered as if it were gold, with the sun shining on it.

As she got closer to where the water met the sand, she could hear talking, then she saw two dolphins talking. She also realized that the dolphins were laying on top of the water and talking about their families. Rebecca decided to swim out and see if they would talk to her. So Rebecca dove into a crystal blue ocean and started to swim for the dolphins. About half-way to the dolphins, Rebecca looked up and noticed that the dolphins had stopped talking and were swimming toward her. Since the dolphins were almost to where Rebecca was in the water, she decided to stay there and wait for the dolphins to get to her. Before the dolphins got there, Rebecca figured out that she could sit on top of the water.

As soon as the dolphins got right in front of her she said, "Hello, my name is Rebecca."

"Well Rebecca, it is very nice to meet you," said the first dolphin, whose name is Summer.

"You look lost. Can we help?" asked the second dolphin, named Autumn.

"Well, I'm a little confused. I don't know where I am, why the animals dress like humans, talk like humans, and why you can lay on top of the water and I can sit on top of the water?" asked Rebecca.

Summer spoke first, "You are on the Island of Animals. Well, in the sea that surrounds the island, and it is a magical island."

"I have never heard of the Island of Animals before. So there are no people here?" asked Rebecca.

"That is right. You are the first human to come here, and the only one here," explained Autumn.

"If you are tired from swimming, we can give you a ride back to the island," offered Summer.

"That would be great," said Rebecca as she climbed onto Summer.

Summer, Autumn, and Rebecca started swimming towards the shore. Rebecca was just having so much fun and the ride to the land was over way too soon.

"Thank you so much, and I hope to see you again soon," said Rebecca as she climbed off.

"We hope to see you again too," replied Summer and Autumn as they swam off.

As Rebecca started walking down a path with palm trees on both sides, she heard voices, and wondered what kind of animal they came from. As she got closer she saw kola bears talking.

Since Rebecca wasn't sure if it was morning or afternoon she just said, "Hi."

"Why hello there, young lady," exclaimed the male kola bear in a low booming voice.

"Hi, my name is Rebecca. What is yours?" Rebecca asked.

"My name is Morton, Morton the Kola," answered the Kola bear. All at once, the female kola came down out of the tree.

29

"Morton, who are you talking too?"

"Her name is Rebecca. She is a visitor here," Morton answered his wife.

"Well, welcome Rebecca. My name is Lexi. I'm Morton's wife," said Lexi as she shook Rebecca's hand.

Lexi's voice was high and squeaked a little when she got excited. "So how long will you be staying here?" asked Lexi.

"I'm not sure. You see I'm dreaming, so when I leave is not really up to me. I leave when I leave," Rebecca told them.

"Well, I hope you enjoy it here for however long you are here," said Lexi.

"Ok, well, it has been nice talking to you, but I would like to look around the island," said Rebecca.

"Have fun then, dear," Lexi responded, as she and Morton waved goodbye to Rebecca.

As Rebecca started off into a forest, she spotted a unicorn. It's mane and tail were every color of the rainbow, and it's body was white. Rebecca stood amazed by this creature, as she just stared at it. The unicorn turned around and asked,

"Well, hello there, and who might you be?"

"Me? I'm-I'm Rebecca," Rebecca stuttered, as she spoke to the unicorn named Isabelle.

"Well Rebecca, I'm Isabelle, and I'm the queen of the Island of Animals."

"Well, it is very nice to meet the queen of such

a beautiful place," said Rebecca, as she stared at the unicorn.

"Rebecca dear, you have been starting at me. Is there something wrong?" asked Isabelle.

"Oh no, nothing, you are just very pretty," Rebecca answered, in an almost whisper.

"Well thank you, let me take you on a tour of my island," said Isabelle, as she got down on the ground so Rebecca could get on her back.

As they went through the woods, Rebecca just sat on Isabelle and was amazed at how green the leaves on the trees were.

"Isabelle do you have seasons here?" Rebecca asked, since in her home land it was autumn.

"We do, we have two season summer and spring," answered Isabelle.

"Those are my favorites back home. Back home we have four seasons," explained Rebecca, and she started to explain to Isabelle how all the seasons work back home.

"Rebecca, I need you to be quiet now. We are about to enter Sentara Valley. They are not mean or violent, but they are very protective of their land. They may come after you, if they hear you talking, thinking you are alone. So let me announce that it is me with a visitor," explained Isabelle. "My Sentaras, I, your Queen Isabelle the unicorn, am coming through with a visitor."

"Isabelle, I think I see one. Are sentaras part horse and part human?" asked Rebecca.

"Yes, they are. Like I said, as long as someone they know announces themselves, they are wonderful creatures," answered Isabelle.

Suddenly, Rebecca heard the sound of really big wings, as she looked up she saw a griffin.

"Isabelle! I-I just saw a griffin!" exclaimed Rebecca, surprised.

"Rebecca, are you ok? You stuttered," asked Isabelle.

"Yes, I'm fine. Just surprised that I saw a half lion-half eagle bird." replied Rebecca.

"That is ok, Rebecca, we just never get visitors here, so seeing a griffin over head is a normal thing for us here," explained Isabelle.

"Sorry, it is just so amazing here. This place is wonderful," said Rebecca.

"I'm very glad that you love it here, Rebecca," said Isabelle.

All at once, a second griffin swooped down and landed right in front of Rebecca and Isabelle.

"Dear Isabelle, my queen," said the griffin as he bowed to her.

"Ah Albert, my adviser, this is Rebecca, a visitor to our island," Isabelle said to Albert.

"Well hello, and welcome to the island Rebecca," said Albert, as he bowed to Rebecca as well.

"Why does Albert bow to me?" Rebecca whispered.

"You are upon the queen's back, anyone who is upon the queen's back is raised to the same stature of the queen, and we bow to them," Albert explained to her.

"Ok, it is kind of nice," replied Rebecca.

"Albert dear, is there something you needed?" the queen asked.

"Yes, my queen, you have a dinner engagement this evening, and I wanted to remind you," Albert answered.

"Oh yes, that is right. I forgot. Well Rebecca, I must drop you off at the beach, so that I can get ready. Albert will stay with you there until Lena arrives to take you to the castle," said Isabella as she started off towards the beach.

"Why will Lena take me to the castle?" Rebecca asked.

"Well you seem like a very nice girl, so I figured that you should have a nice supper, and a comfortable place to sleep tonight," answered the queen.

"Oh, well, thank you very much," replied Rebecca.

She slid off the queen's back and bowed to her. Albert and Rebecca were sitting on the sand when Rebecca gasped, because she saw a wolf.

"Don't worry, that is Lena," Albert assured her.

The wolf trotted over to them and introduced herself.

"Hello Rebecca, I'm Lena. I'm here to take you to the castle," Lena said, as she shook Rebecca's hand.

"I'm pleased to meet you, Lena," replied Rebecca.

"Albert, you may go, and perform your duties. I will take Rebecca to the castle and see to her needs the rest of the night."

Once Rebecca and Lena reached the castle, supper was ready and laid out, also there were about a dozen other animals seated.

"Come," said Lena. "Come sit, and eat with us."

Rebecca sat down very timidly next to a panther named Joshua. On the other side of her was a panda bear named Allison. Allison reached her paw over and put it around Rebecca's back

"It is ok, we are all nice here."

Before Rebecca could say anything back, Lena stood up to speak.

"Hello everyone, and thank you for coming to dinner. I would like to introduce you to our very first guest, Rebecca," said Lena, as she raised her paw towards Rebecca.

Rebecca stood up on shaky legs and said, "Hello, I'm Rebecca, and I'm thirteen."

"Welcome Rebecca!" everyone shouted together.

As soon as they were done saying welcome, Rebecca sat down fast. After the prayer was given by Albert, the food was passed. After dessert, Joshua and Allison told Lena to help clean up and that they would take Rebecca to her room for the night.

They walked down a long hallway that had paintings of all the past queens going back through the years.

"This is called the Hall of Queens, these are paintings of all our past queens, going back almost three hundred years," explained Allison.

"Wow! I would of guessed two hundred years," exclaimed Rebecca, "I guess animals live longer here than where I come from."

"Well, how long do unicorns live where you live?" asked Joshua.

"We don't have unicorns where I live," replied Rebecca.

"Oh, well, unicorns live for one hundred years but they only serve as queens for thirty five to fifty years," explained Allison.

"Wow, that is very interesting," said Rebecca, "How much longer is Isabelle going to be queen?"

"She has thirty-four years till she reaches thirty-five years. She has only been queen for a year, but we love her," answered Joshua.

"Here we are. This will be your room for tonight, if you need anything just let us know. My room is right next door," explained Allison.

"That is wonderful. Then I will see you two at breakfast," said Rebecca, then went into her room.

Once inside, Rebecca walked over to huge oak cabinet with a cherry finish, in it she found a silk night gown and she put it on. Once she brushed her teeth with the tooth brush she found in her private bathroom, she climbed under the blankets and fell asleep.

When Rebecca woke up she saw the sun starting to rise. Around seven o'clock, Allison came to let Rebecca know Albert would be by in half an hour to get her for breakfast.

"Rebecca, I thought I would let you know that in half an hour Albert will be here to get you for breakfast," said Allison then left to help cook breakfast.

"Thank you, Allison," replied Rebecca.

Once Allison left Rebecca looked in the oak cabinet for clothes to put on, and she found a light purple jumper, with a white shirt, white socks, and light purple dress shoes.

"I can't believe this. These are all my size and the jumper and shoes are my favorite color," said Rebecca, as she got dressed.

When Albert came to get Rebecca for breakfast, she asked him, "Albert, how come the clothes I found in the cabinet were my favorite colors and just my size?"

"This is a magical island, my dear, that is how magic works, my dear," answered Albert.

"So cool! This place is so cool," said Rebecca with an excited squeak in her voice.

After breakfast, the queen told Rebecca she had business she had to get to, but Allison and Joshua would take care of her today. Allison, Joshua, and Rebecca went out into the forest, and Joshua taught her how to climb trees, Allison had her taste bamboo, which Rebecca didn't like.

"I don't know how you eat this, Allison, it is awful," exclaimed Rebecca, as she spit out the bamboo.

"It is just what I always ate. It is what pandas eat," explained Allison.

"So Joshua, what do panthers eat?" Rebecca asked.

"We eat meat mostly, but I have grown to like berries too," replied Joshua.

As the three headed towards the beach, the Island of Animals started to fade. Rebecca had just enough time to say, "Good-bye Joshua, good-bye Allison." They turned to say goodbye, but she was gone.

As she woke up at Miss Kathy's house, she looked out the window in the room she shared with another girl, and saw that the sun was rising over the mountain.

Chapter 6
New Life

Rebecca got up and woke her roommate, then they got dressed and went downstairs to breakfast. Since they were an hour early, Miss Kathy asked them to help make breakfast, and to set the table. Forty-five minutes later, the rest of the children came down for breakfast. Once the food was on the table, they said grace and started to eat.

"After breakfast, I would like to see Rebecca in my office," announced Miss Kathy.

As soon as Rebecca heard that her stomach was in knots, and she couldn't eat anymore. "*What did I do? Am I in trouble? What is going in?*" Rebecca thought.

Once breakfast was over, a group of kids started to clean up as Miss Kathy and Rebecca went to Miss Kathy's office. Once inside, Miss Kathy closed the door and told Rebecca to sit down.

"Rebecca you are not in trouble. I have some

wonderful news for you. Joy and Wayne want to adopt you," Miss Kathy said smiling.

"Wow, I didn't think I would get picked being thirteen and all!" exclaimed Rebecca, almost jumping out of the chair.

"Now it will take some time for all the paper work to get done, but you can move in with them tomorrow. They will be here today to take you out to lunch to welcome you to their family," explained Miss Kathy.

At about twelve o'clock that day, Joy and Wayne came to take Rebecca out to lunch.

"Rebecca, where would you like to eat?" Joy asked her when they got into Joy and Wayne's SUV.

"I don't know, I'm really hungry for a hamburger," Rebecca said as she buckled herself in.

"Well, that settles it, then I know a great place that makes the best hamburgers ever," said Wayne, as he started the vehicle.

"Where is that?" asked Rebecca.

"Our house!" exclaimed Joy and Wayne at the same time. "Wayne makes the best hamburgers ever," said Joy.

"Joy makes the best French fries and milkshakes," as they started towards the house Rebecca would call home.

On the way to the house, Rebecca asked, "Not that I'm ungrateful or anything, but why did you pick me and not someone younger?"

"Well, when we saw your age we figured you would think you would never get adopted since you are thirteen," explained Joy.

"Then when we met you and spent that day with you, we fell in love with you," said Wayne.

"We love you, Rebecca, we picked you cause we wanted you, not someone younger," said Joy, as they pulled into the driveway.

As soon as Rebecca got out of the SUV, Joy and Wayne put one arm around her and walked her into the house. Once inside Rebecca wanted to know what she could do to help make lunch.

"Rebecca, you don't need to help. You can go up and check out your new room. It is up the stairs, second room on the right," said Joy.

"No, please, I want to see it for the first time tomorrow when I move in. So can I help? I love to cook," Rebecca asked.

After the burgers and French fries were done, Joy asked Rebecca, "So sweetie, what is your favorite ice cream flavor? I got four different flavors since I wasn't sure what you'll like."

"I like vanilla bean, or plain vanilla is fine too," said Rebecca.

"I have vanilla bean. Wayne told me he thought you would like that. He likes it too," said Joy, as she got out the ice cream to make the milkshakes.

Once the milkshakes were ready they sat down at

the table to eat. After Wayne said grace they started to eat. When lunch was just about over Rebecca said, "So I have a question for both of you."

"Sure sweetie, what is your question?" said Joy.

"So when can I call you mom and dad?" Rebecca asked.

"Whenever you want to, Princess," answered Wayne.

"Ok I think I might wait for a little bit." Said Rebecca with a big smile.

After they cleaned up from lunch, they took Rebecca back to Miss Kathy's house. They hugged and kissed her goodbye and told her they would see her tomorrow.

"So where did they take you for lunch? You were gone awhile," Miss Kathy asked.

"They took me to their house, since I was hungry for a hamburger, because Wayne makes the best hamburgers ever. Joy made French fries and milkshakes. It was wonderful," said Rebecca.

Before she went to her room to pack, she asked Miss Kathy if she could call Joy and Wayne because she forgot the thank them for lunch.

"Sure, come to my office and we will make the call," said Miss Kathy.

Once Miss Kathy dialed the number she gave the phone to Rebecca. Joy answered the phone.

"Hello."

"Hi Joy, this is Rebecca, I forgot to thank you and Wayne for lunch today. Sorry I forgot, so thank you for lunch. It was very good," explained Rebecca.

"Oh, well, you're very welcome sweetie. You don't need to be sorry. Everyone forgets from time to time. We will see you tomorrow. Goodbye," said Joy, then she hung up the phone.

Rebecca told Miss Kathy thank you, then went up to her room to pack her things. When she got up to her room Rebecca wanted to wear the outfit Joy and Wayne had gotten her, but since it was March it was too cold for shorts.

"I can't wear the shorts but I can wear the shirt," thought Rebecca, as she laid out the shirt with the rest of her outfit for tomorrow.

By the time supper was ready Rebecca was almost done packing. She went downstairs to eat supper with her foster brothers and sisters for the last time. Once they were all seated, and they had said grace, Miss Kathy made and announcement.

"Boys and girls, tomorrow morning we will have a farewell party for Rebecca. She is getting adopted. So for breakfast we will have something special.:

It was hard for Rebecca to fall asleep, because as long as she could remember she had lived with Miss Kathy, and tomorrow she would be in a new home with new parents. She finally got to sleep and then before she knew it her roommate was waking her up.

"Rebecca, I can't believe this is the last time I will be waking you up," said her roommate Hope.

"I know Hope, it is hard to think I won't be waking you up anymore either," said Rebecca, as she and Hope hugged each other and cried.

"Don't worry, I'm sure Joy and Wayne will bring me back to see you and let me have you over to visit me."

Everyone went downstairs for breakfast, the special breakfast was cinnamon rolls. Once everyone sat down and grace was said, they all had breakfast together one last time. Once breakfast was over, Miss Kathy told them the dishes could wait till Rebecca left. They told Rebecca how much they would miss her, and what they liked most about her. About ten o'clock Joy and Wayne came to take Rebecca home with them.

After Rebecca said her goodbyes and hugged everyone, she hugged and kissed Miss Kathy and said, "Thank you for being a great foster mom. I love you."

Then she walked out the door with her new parents. As she turned around one more time, Wayne told her to take her time as he took her suitcase to put it in the SUV. Rebecca saw everyone in the windows or on the porch waving goodbye. As tears filled her eyes she waved goodbye then got into the SUV to go home with her new parents. Once home they had left over hamburgers for lunch, then Joy and Wayne helped Rebecca unpack.

"I'm not sure how much of my summer clothes

will fit. Some were tight last summer already," said Rebecca.

"That is ok, we can buy you any clothes you need for summer," said Joy, "I see you are wearing the shirt we bought you when we spent that day with you."

"Yes, I love it a lot," said Rebecca as she sat down on the bed to look at her new room. "I love the room. It is just so quiet here," said Rebecca.

"We are glad you like your room, don't worry you will get used to it being quiet."

After a supper of pizza with ham and broccoli that night, Joy and Wayne both put Rebecca to bed.

After they said goodnight, Rebecca said "Good night mom and dad. I love you."

That night, Rebecca went to sleep. That night feeling safe and loved by two very special people. She just couldn't wait for her new life to begin.

The End

Printed in the United States
By Bookmasters